Paddington
King of the Castle

First published in paperback as *Paddington Rules the Waves* in Great Britain
by HarperCollins Children's Books in 2008
New edition published in 2009
Board book edition published in 2016
This edition published as part of a set in 2017

1 3 5 7 9 10 8 6 4 2

ISBN: 978-0-00-796826-8

HarperCollins Children's Books is a division of HarperCollins Publishers Ltd.

Text copyright © Michael Bond 2008
Illustrations copyright © R. W. Alley 2008

Visit our website at: www.harpercollins.co.uk

Printed in China

Michael Bond

Paddington
King of the Castle

Illustrated by R. W. Alley

HarperCollins *Children's Books*

Nothing much goes on at the seaside that seagulls don't know about. So when Paddington went down to the beach early one morning, he soon had company.

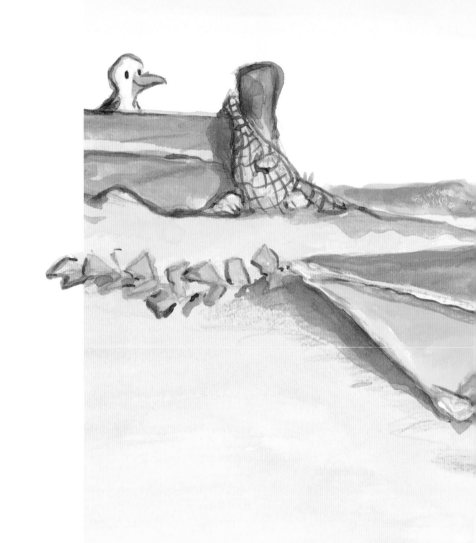

"It's a bear," cried seagull number 1, "and he's digging up *our* beach!"

"He's made a sand castle," said seagull number 2. "Look how pleased he is."

"Now he's lost his bucket," said seagull number 3. "I could have told him that would happen. Screech! Screech!"

"I think he must be learning to fly," said seagull number 4, as Paddington began playing with his kite.

"He's much too heavy
for that," screeched
seagull number 5.

"What did I tell you?"
it cried, as seagull
number 6 joined them.

As Paddington was looking out to sea for his kite, seagull number 7 flew in. "Look!" it cried. "He's got a bun in his pocket!"

While Paddington struggled with his deck chair, seagull number 8 landed. "I'm hungry," it screeched. "Shall I try giving the bun a peck and see what happens?"

"Wait until there are more of us," hissed seagull number 9.

Sure enough, a moment
later, seagull number 10
arrived. "Here goes!"
called one at the back.
And they all made a dive.

"Seagulls don't know everything," said Paddington, when they had gone. "I always keep a marmalade sandwich under my hat, just in case!"

Look out for more fantastic books about Paddington!

Paddington
at the Palace

Michael
Bond

Illustrated by
R. W. Alley

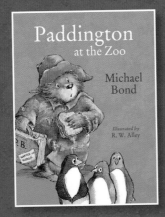

Paddington
at the Zoo

Michael
Bond

Illustrated by
R. W. Alley

Michael Bond

Paddington
at the Tower

Illustrated by
R. W. Alley

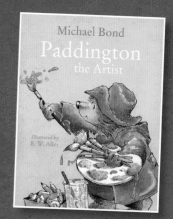

Michael Bond

Paddington
the Artist

Illustrated by
R. W. Alley

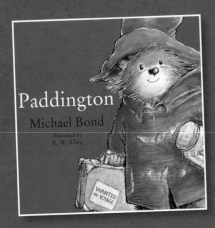

Paddington

Michael Bond

Illustrated by
R. W. Alley

WANTED on VOYAGE

Paddington
in the
Garden

Michael Bond

Illustrated by
R. W. Alley

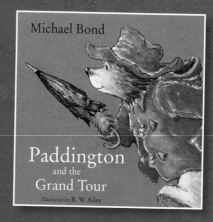

Michael Bond

Paddington
and the
Grand Tour

Illustrated by R. W. Alley

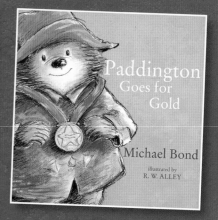

Paddington
Goes for
Gold

Michael Bond

illustrated by
R. W. ALLEY

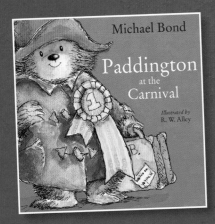

Michael Bond

Paddington
at the
Carnival

Illustrated by
R. W. Alley

Michael Bond

Paddington
and the
Christmas
Surprise

Illustrated by R. W. ALLEY

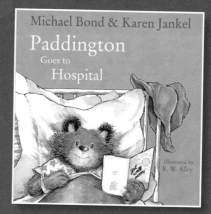

Michael Bond & Karen Jankel

Paddington
Goes to
Hospital

Illustrated by
R. W. Alley

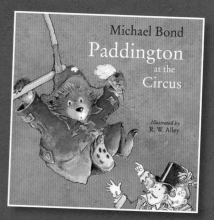

Michael Bond

Paddington
at the
Circus

Illustrated by
R. W. Alley

HarperCollins *Children's Books*